W9-AYX-786

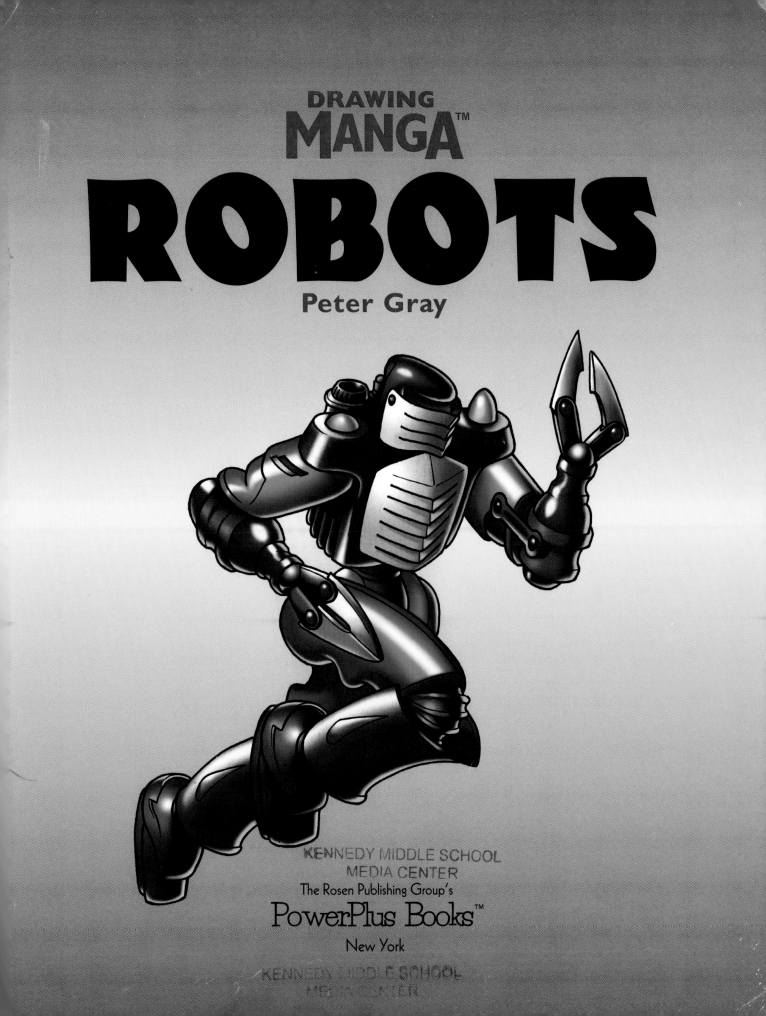

DRAWING
MANGA™
ROBOTS

Peter Gray

The Rosen Publishing Group's

PowerPlus Books™

New York

Published in 2006 by The Rosen Publishing Group,
Inc.
29 East 21st Street, New York, NY 10010

First Edition

Editor: Alex Woolf
Designer: Jane Hawkins
Artwork: Peter Gray
Digital coloring: David Stevenson

Library of Congress Cataloging-in-Publication Data
Gray, Peter C., 1969-
Robots / Peter Gray.— 1st ed.
p. cm. — (Drawing Manga)
Includes index.
ISBN 1-4042-3332-6 (library binding)
1. Robots in art—Juvenile literature. 2. Comic
books, strips, etc.—Japan—Technique—Juvenile
literature. 3. Cartooning—Technique—Juvenile
literature. I. Title: Robots. II. Title. III. Series.
NC1764.8.R63G73 2006
741.5—dc22
2005011760

Manufactured in United States of America

Contents

Introduction   4

Materials   5

Basic Techniques   6

Composition   6

Color Theory   8

Light and Shade   10

Coloring   12

Perspective   14

Creating Magnus   15

Two-point Perspective   18

Giant Robot   19

Projects   22

X-O-Dus   22

Designing a Robot   26

Developing the Robot   28

Glossary   30

Further Information   31

Index   32

Introduction

Manga comics are full of robots, also known as mechas. These towering hulks of high-powered metal can fly, swim, fire weapons, and fight epic battles with their enemies.

Most manga robots are humanoid, or based on the human shape. Unlike human characters, though, you can create your robot characters with all sorts of fun gadgets or weapons. You can even give them wings!

The other great news is that drawing manga robots is a lot easier than drawing humans. If you can draw blocks and circles, then you're already halfway there.

How to Draw Manga Robots has plenty of projects to get you started and to inspire your imagination. Don't be put off by the slick look of the artwork produced by professional artists. It isn't that hard to achieve once you know some of the tricks of the trade.

The ability to draw is the most important skill for any aspiring manga artist to develop, and this will only come about if you keep practicing. All this effort will pay off eventually, and you will notice how much more inventive and interesting your drawings become.

Magnus

This is Magnus, a robot with a heart of gold — literally! He might be a lump of metal, but he has an intelligently programmed brain that can make you believe he really has a sensitive soul. Magnus will be modeling for us later in the book. He will also pop up from time to time with drawing tips and suggestions.

Materials

For the exercises in this book, it will help you to use a hard pencil for sketching light guidelines and a soft pencil to make the final lines of each of your drawings distinct. Pencils are graded by hardness. Number-one pencils are the softest and make the darkest lines. Number-three pencils are the hardest, making the lightest lines. The most commonly used pencil is the number two. Get a number-two mechanical pencil if at all possible, since this will produce a constant fine line for your final image. Using a mechanical pencil will avoid the need for sharpening.

You'll need an eraser too, since you'll have to sketch a lot of rough lines to get your drawing right. Once you are satisfied with your drawing, you will want to get rid of those lines using a clean eraser.

When it comes to coloring, colored pencils are easiest to use. You might want to start with them. Once you have developed your skills, you can try felt-tip pens and watercolor paints. You also do not need to get special paper to create your drawings, unless you decide to work with paints. In that case you will want to get a thicker paper that won't wrinkle when it gets wet.

Basic Techniques

Before we get started on drawing robots, we're going to take a look at some of the basic rules of picture design and color theory.

Composition

Composition is one of the first things to consider when making a picture. It's all about where you place the elements you want to include in your picture. Here we're going to look at the most basic rules of composition.

Portrait format
A picture that is taller than it is wide is known as portrait format. The two pictures on this page show Magnus in a portrait-shaped frame.

1 Bad placement
When people are taking photographs, you'd be surprised how often they make the mistake of placing the focal point of the picture right in the middle of the frame. The same thing can happen when someone draws a picture. Here Magnus is placed too low. His head is the focal point and it sits halfway down the frame, as marked by the green line. There is too much empty space above his head and he looks like he's going to drop out of the bottom of the picture.

2 Vertical placement
The height of an object within the frame is known as the vertical placement. This picture shows good vertical placement. Magnus fills the frame nicely, without too much empty space and without having any of his body parts cropped.

Landscape format

The pictures in these frames are wider than they are tall. Called landscape format, it is normally used by photographers and artists when they want to capture a wide area of scenery.

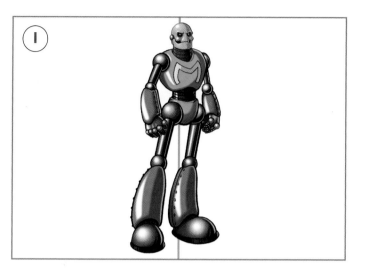

1 Horizontal placement

The position of an object along the width of the frame is known as the horizontal placement. Here Magnus has been placed centrally. Although this can sometimes work well, more often than not it looks boring and should be avoided.

2 Golden section

It is generally accepted that pictures work better when the objects are placed to the left or right of center. The ancient Greeks worked out a geometric equation known as the golden section, and today's artists still use it. In simple terms it states that objects should be placed just over a third of the way in from the picture's edge.

3 Moving left or right

Placing Magnus to the left or right and placing him roughly on the lines of the golden section immediately makes for a more interesting picture.

Color Theory

The colors you use for a picture will have a major impact on its final look and feel. Here Magnus is proudly modeling some simple color schemes.

1 Primary colors
Red, blue, and yellow are the basic colors from which all other colors can be mixed. They are called primary colors. If you can afford only three colored pencils, pens, or paints, go for these colors.

2 Secondary colors
Green, purple, and orange are called secondary colors. Each one is a combination of two primary colors. In these three pictures, the two primary colors of Magnus's limbs are mixed together to make the secondary color of his chest armor.

3 Full spectrum
The three primary and three secondary colors make up the full spectrum of pure bright colors. Putting all of these colors together in one picture can be overpowering, so it's usually wise to limit the number of colors you use.

4 Tints and shades

When colors have white added to them, they are called tints and will look pale. When colors have black added to them, they are called shades and look darker. Here the same color has been used for each of Magnus's body parts. For the picture on the left, white was added to produce a pastel version. For the second picture, black was added to produce a darker version.

5 Complementary colors

Some colors go together better than others. Every primary color has a secondary color as its complementary color, which is a combination of the other two primaries. For example, red is complemented by green (blue plus yellow). Here Magnus is dressed in various tints and shades of blue and orange (yellow plus red).

6 Harmonious color schemes

To help convince you that you don't always need to use lots of different colors, this picture has been colored using only tints and shades of green. There is certainly no chance of any colors clashing here!

Light and Shade

To use color effectively, you need to understand how light and shade affect an object.

1 Daytime shadows

Light is hitting these shapes from the upper right. The surfaces facing toward the light appear brighter than the parts that face away. The parts facing away will not be completely black, however, because light also bounces off other objects to faintly illuminate, or light, these areas.

2 Nighttime shadows

At night, when objects are lit directly from man-made light sources, there may be no light reflecting off other things. The parts of an object that face away from the light source can blend into the darkness.

3 Simple shading

First decide which direction the light is coming from, then lightly shade the surfaces of your picture that aren't facing the light directly. In this picture, the light is coming from top right again. Use a very soft pencil, holding it at an angle but without pressing down too heavily.

4 Creating shadows

Some parts of an object like this robot will block out the light from other parts. An arm might cast a shadow on a leg, for instance. Keeping the light direction in mind, imagine where various body parts might cast shadows on other parts and shade those areas darker.

5 Hidden areas

Some parts of the robot are tucked away, like the little crevices under close-fitting joints. Shade these parts more heavily.

6 Angles

Polish your picture by working across each body part and imagining the different ways that light falls on it. Shade the parts to different degrees, depending on the angle of each part in relation to the direction of light.

7 Adding backgrounds

Here is the finished picture against two different backgrounds. A gray background makes the lighter areas stand out more and helps show the effects of reflected light around the left and lower edges of the body parts. If you put the same drawing on a black background and remove the reflected light, the edges blend in with the background completely.

Coloring

Here the artist used artist's-quality marker pens to color Magnus, but you can get similar effects with ordinary felt-tip pens.

1 Robot color swatches
Magnus is really only five colors. They are gray, blue, green, yellow, and gold. To show how light falls on him (from top left), we also need to use darker shades of each of these colors, so you'll need felt-tips in the different shades you can see here.

2 Adding the color
First use your darker shades. The colors you need are shown next to the picture. Apply them to the areas facing away from the light and to areas that are in the shadow of other parts of the body.

3 Larger areas
Now you can color the bigger areas using lighter colors. When you do this, leave some strips of white. This will have the effect of making the surfaces look shiny.

4 Smaller parts

Continue to add color using the swatches next to the picture to guide you. Notice how the artist used different grays to enhance the shine patterns on the metalwork.

5 Final color

Once you've finished with your felt-tips, you can clean up your picture with some white ink and a fine brush. Use these to blot out any color that has bled over the lines and to add highlights to the metalwork. Finally, add a glow of reflected light to the right-hand side of the picture. Draw thin strips of white on the head, chest, and arm. Let this ink dry, then use a fine-nibbed felt-tip pen to color these strips light blue.

Perspective

In this section we will look at perspective, which is the angle, height, and distance from which you view an object. Then we will try out some projects that use the techniques we've learned.

Anything you draw will be affected by the angle and height of your viewpoint. With the skeleton framework of a human at a three-quarter angle, we can see that it looks different depending on our eye level.

1 Middle perspective
The horizontal blue line represents our eye level. The red lines help us to see that all the parts of the body that are above our eye level appear to slope down as they recede. Those below our eye line slope up. All of these angles converge at a single point on the horizon.

①

2 High perspective
Here the horizontal blue line shows that the same skeleton is now below our eye level, so all parts of the body appear to slope upward as they get farther away from us.

②

3 Low perspective
If we look at the figure so it's above our eye level, all parts of the body appear to slope down to the left.

③

Creating Magnus

This is a three-quarter view of Magnus the robot with lines added to help you get the perspective right.

Step 1
Draw three oval shapes for the body parts as shown. Add a curved vertical guideline to each body part, then draw a horizontal guideline across the head. Notice how the ends curve downward. Copy the angles of the three sloping perspective lines.

Step 2
Add the arm and leg bones. Notice that the perspective lines run through the joints.

Step 3
Make the shape of the upper arms and legs by drawing different-sized circles connected by parallel lines. Outline the large boots, too.

Step 4
Now outline the metalwork of the forearms, hands, and lower legs.

Step 5

Draw the outline of the metal suit surrounding the chest and hips. Work on the main features of the head and add a bit more detail to the lower legs and feet.

5

6

Step 6

Add further detail to his face and eyes. Draw in the rows of horizontal lines down the front of the body to create a subframe made up of metal discs. Add the letter M to the chest and work on the detail of the giant hands. The thick metal fingers have large circular joints.

Step 7

Pick out all your good lines to form the shape of your final drawing and go over these in heavy pencil. Now go over all your final lines again using a black felt-tip pen. Finally, study the picture carefully to see if you've missed any little details.

7

⑧

Step 8

When the pen ink dries, erase all the pencil lines that formed your original framework to leave a clean drawing of Magnus. Notice how I've added lots of thin vertical lines to the discs that make up the torso. Now color him in.

Two-point Perspective

Knowledge of one-point perspective is all you need for many of the figures you will draw. However, if you are tackling a figure that is very solid and blocky, like the robot featured next, it will help you understand a bit about two-point perspective.

1–3 Simple cube

These diagrams show the effects of perspective on a simple solid cube. You'll notice that the angles recede in two directions. This is two-point perspective. The two points form a horizontal line known as the horizon, or eye line. For the first picture, the eye line is above the cube. For the second picture, it's below the shape, and for the third, it's in the middle.

4 Stacked cubes

If we stack these cubes on top of each other, we have a shape that could form the basis of a three-dimensional figure that is drawn in perspective.

5 Robot blocks

This diagram shows the main blocks that make up the body of the robot we will be drawing next. Because the head and chest are at a different angle from the hips and legs, the points at which the angles of the body come together are different. They still meet on the horizon, though. This is always the case with objects that stand level with the ground.

Giant Robot

Before you start drawing, take a look at
the finished character on the next page
so you know what you're aiming for.

Step 1
Start with the basic shapes that
form the head, chest, and hips.
Like Magnus, the chest is much
larger than the head and hips.
Notice how the vertical guideline
is in a different position on the
hips, as the figure is twisting.

Step 2
Although this robot doesn't really have bones and
joints, drawing them will help you work out the
positions of the robotic limbs and where they
bend. Add some perspective lines to help draw the
legs. The leg to the right of your picture is farther
away, so it appears shorter.

Step 3
Turn the chest into a cube
and draw a rectangular box
around the hips. Use a ruler if
it helps. Copy the blocky
shape of the upper legs,
making the nearest leg
thicker. Draw semicircles
for knee joints.

Step 4
Add more blocks to form the
rough shape of the lower legs
and the robot's arms.

Step 5

Start to polish your robot's shape. Make the chest more angular, turn the waist into a narrow, curvy tube, and add a power pack to the robot's back. Copy the rest of the metalwork and make the basic shapes of the hands. To draw the giant outstretched hand, start with the framework for the finger bones, then add in the palm and the lines for the fingers.

5

Step 6

Add the segmented parts of the fingers. Add details to the shape of the hand that is on the right in the picture. Copy all the panels, or plates, on the chest and draw the lines on the legs and the treads on the feet. Add in the helicopter here, too.

The helicopter gives the picture a sense of scale. We can now see that this robot is about the same size as a skyscraper.

6

Step 7

Go over all your good lines in heavy pencil, then in black felt-tip pen.

Step 8

When the ink is dry, erase all your pencil marks. Now you can enjoy adding color. Add some strips of white to make the metal look like it's reflecting the light. The helicopter is bright green so it stands out against the colors of the robot's body.

7

8

Projects

By this point, you should feel fairly sure about drawing manga robots. Now here are some challenging projects to sink your artistic teeth into. Once you've mastered how to draw these robots, you should be well equipped to release any number of your own mechanical creations into the manga world.

X-O-Dus—Head

The mecha X-O-Dus is heavily armored and equipped for close-combat fighting.

Step 1
Begin with a long vertical line, then draw a smooth arch across the top. Copy the shapes that make up its jawline and chin. Draw a horizontal line and then two vertical lines going up from the corners of the chin. Join up those lines with curves that follow the lines of the jaw.

Step 2
Now add the spikes and draw another horizontal line just below the crown of the helmet. Join the ends of that line to the sides of the helmet at the point where your curved lines end. Within the rectangle in the middle of the brow, draw a hexagon and a diamond shape.

Step 3
Break up the curve of the jaw and chin area. Add extra lines inside your new jawline to make the picture look more three-dimensional. Some more straight lines inside the spikes on the sides of the head and the forehead hexagon will add to the effect. Add horizontal lines to the visor. Draw two circles that will be left white for its eyes.

Step 4
X-O-Dus provides good shading and coloring practice because its helmet is made up of flat and curved surfaces, all of which reflect light differently.

X-O-Dus—Figure

Step 1
X-O-Dus is basically human in shape but broader and with big joints. You're only blocking in rough shapes at the moment, but try to get the proportions right.

Step 2
The body shape here is more like armor than flesh. Shoulders, hips, and limbs are all huge except for its upper arms, which have no armor because they need to be able to move freely.

When shading, notice that X-O-Dus has a dull metallic surface with deep shadows and bright highlights. You might find your eraser very useful as you finish the drawing.

Step 3
You have to think three-dimensionally and try to show, in a few simple lines, the solidity of this powerful robot. Just like its helmet, X-O-Dus's body is a mixture of curves and angles. Erase your guidelines as you go so that you don't get confused.

Step 4

Adding the details to X-O-Dus will give it that hard, military look. Don't forget to draw its joints. They help you imagine the way the robot moves in battle and add to its scariness.

④

⑤

Step 5

When shading and coloring, remember to think about where the light is coming from. Leaving the paper white in places can be very effective. You can also use white paint to add highlights at the end.

X-O-Dus—In Action

Step 1

Here's a tricky picture of X-O-Dus. The head is seen from the front, but its shoulders are at an angle, and it is swinging its right arm back while its left arm comes forward. When you run, your arms and legs work opposite to each other, so draw the right leg coming forward and the left leg bent under it.

Step 2

This is similar to the last drawing of X-O-Dus on pages 23–24, except that you see less of its torso. As you add the hand shapes, you'll notice that its left hand overlaps its leg, but you can erase the guidelines underneath.

Step 3

Now you are ready to sharpen up the shapes and sort out the details. Hands and feet are important, as always. Work on the angular quality of the legs, too.

Step 4

Those all-important mechanical details will finish off the picture. This is a sophisticated drawing, so pat yourself on the back when you've got it to this stage. When you're happy with it, you're ready to have fun with the coloring.

Designing a Robot

All sorts of everyday objects can provide inspiration for drawing robots. Here are some objects that might be found lying around the home. They are all quite ordinary things, but any of their features or geometric qualities could be incorporated into the design of a new robot character.

box cutter

binoculars

electric whisk

hairdryer

computer mouse

kettle

watering can

perfume bottle

soap dispenser

pliers

vacuum cleaner

Junk Robot

Here are some of the household objects from the previous page assembled into a very rough robotic form. Notice, for instance, the giant binoculars that form the power pack on the back. This design still needs a lot of work, since the last thing a manga super mecha wants is to look as if he's made from giant kettles and vacuum cleaner parts. Before you turn this page and find out how to develop him further, try the following exercise.

Exercise

Find some objects that interest you around your home or pictures of objects in books. They might be airplane parts, engines, tools, electronic items, or anything else that could be made to look robotic. Build up a few pages of small sketches of these items, then try using all or part of each object to assemble a robot of your own.

Developing the Robot

To bring our collection of junk to life requires a few more stages of development.

Step 1
Here we are using a chunky human form for the robot.

Step 2
Because the body type we are drawing is very bulky, the robot could easily look cumbersome, so you'll want to choose a dynamic pose.

Step 3
A mechanical version of the running human is now easy to draw.

Step 4
Next build up the robot part by part, basing the design on your sketches of the junk robot from the previous page. This time, however, we will only use the household objects as an inspiration and instead invent new parts to suit our machine.

Step 5

To disguise your source material even more, and to give the drawing more of a manga feel, add some extra details like the slatted metal visor and chest plate. When you're happy with your robot, go over it in black pen. Once the ink is dry, erase all remaining pencil marks.

Step 6

Before coloring your own robot, you might want to flip back to pages 10–11 to see how you might approach shading to give him the appearance of solidity.

Deciding on the final shape of your robot's parts can mean a lot of redrawing, but going over your final lines in heavy pencil and erasing all the mistakes will make your final design much clearer.

Glossary

angular (AN-gyuh-lur) Having angles or sharp corners.

complementary (kom-plih-MEN-tuh-ree) Combining well with something else.

converge (kun-VERJ) To join.

crevices (KREH-vis-ez) Narrow cracks or openings.

cumbersome (KUM-ber-sum) Difficult to move.

dynamic (dy-NA-mik) Full of energy.

enhance (in-HANTS) To improve.

framework (FRAYM-werk) Basic structure.

geometric (jee-uh-MEH trik) Following the laws of geometry, the study of the properties and relationships of points, lines, angles, curves, surfaces, and solids.

golden section (GOL-den SEK-shun) The proportion of a straight line that occurs when you divide the line in two so that the relationship of the whole line to the larger part is equal to that of the larger part to the smaller part.

harmonious (har-MOH-nee-us) Having a pleasing combination of parts or colors.

hexagon (HEK-suh-gon) A two-dimensional shape with six sides.

highlights (HY-lyts) Areas of very light tone in a painting that provide contrast or the appearance of illumination.

horizontal (hor-ih-ZON-tul) Parallel to the horizon.

humanoid (HYOO-muh-noyd) A robot or alien with the basic shape of a human being.

joints (JOYNTS) The parts of a body where bones are connected.

manga (MAHN-guh) The exact translation of this word is "irresponsible pictures." Manga is a Japanese style of animation that has been popular since the 1960s.

mechas (MEH-kuhz) A Japanese shortening of the English word "mechanical." Mechas can be anything of a mechanical nature, including weapons, advanced body armor, and robots.

parallel (PAR-uh-lel) Having to do with lines or planes that are always the same distance apart and therefore never meet.

pastel (pa-STEL) A pale, soft color.

perspective (per-SPEK-tiv) In drawing, changing the relative size and appearance of objects to allow for the effects of distance.

proportions (pruh-POR-shunz) The relationships between the parts of a whole figure.

recede (ree-SEED) To get farther away from the observer.

segmented (SEG-men-ted) Divided into segments.

swatches (SWACH-ez) Things used as samples.

torso (TOR-soh) The upper part of the human body, not including the head and arms.

vertical (VER-tih-kul) Upright, or at a right angle to the horizon.

visor (VY-zer) The hinged front part of a helmet, made of a transparent material and designed for the wearer to look through.

Further Information

Books

The Art of Drawing Manga by Ben Krefta (Arcturus, 2003)

How to Draw Manga: A Step-by-Step Guide by Katy Coope (Scholastic, 2002)

Mecha Mania: How to Draw the Battling Robots, Cool Spaceships, and Military Vehicles of Japanese Comics by Christopher Hart (Watson-Guptill Publications, 2002)

Step-by-Step Manga by Ben Krefta (Scholastic, 2004)

Web Sites

Due to the changing nature of Internet links, PowerKids Press has developed an online list of Web sites related to the subject of this book. This site is updated regularly. Please use this link to access the list:

www.powerkidslinks.com/dman/robots

'Bye everyone! I hope you had fun learning how to draw manga.

Index

A
armor, 8, 23
arms, 10, 13, 15, 19, 23, 25

B
bones, 15, 19–20

C
chest, 13, 16, 18–20, 29
chin, 22
color, 5, 8–9, 12–13, 21–22, 24–25, 29

D
designing, 26–29

E
eraser, use of, 5, 17, 21, 23, 25, 29
eye line, 14, 18
eyes, 22

F
feet, 16, 25
felt-tip pen, use of, 5, 8, 12–13, 16, 21, 29
fingers, 16, 20
framework, 14, 20, 30

G
golden section, 7, 30
guidelines, 15, 19, 23, 25

H
hands, 15, 20, 25
head, 6, 13, 16, 18–19, 25
helmet, 22–23
highlights, 13, 22–24, 30
hips, 16, 18–19, 23
human form, 4, 14, 23, 28

I
inking, 13

J
jaw or jawline, 22
joints, 11, 15–16, 19, 23–24, 30

K
knees, 19

L
landscape format, 7
legs, 10, 15–16, 18–19, 25
light, 10–13, 21–22, 24

M
manga, 4, 29, 30
metalwork, 13, 15, 20

P
paint, 5, 8, 24
paper, 5, 24
pencil, use of, 5, 8, 16, 21, 29
perspective, 14–21, 30
   one-point, 14
   two-point, 18
placement, 6
portrait format, 6
power pack, 20, 27

S
shades, 9, 12
shading, 10–11, 22, 24, 29
shadows, 10, 12, 23
shine patterns, 12–13, 21
shoulders, 23, 25
skeleton, 14

T
three-quarter view, 14–15
tints, 9
torso, 17, 25, 30

V
visor, 22, 29, 30

W
waist, 20
weapons, 4